PARALLEL TO LIFE

ESSAY SERIES 45

Canada

Guernica Editions Inc. acknowledges the support of
The Canada Council for the Arts.
Guernica Editions Inc. acknowledges the support of
the Ontario Arts Council.
Guernica Editions Inc. acknowledges the financial support of the
Government of Canada through the Book Publishing Industry
Development Program (BPIDP).

ANDRÉ ROY

PARALLEL TO LIFE

A NOTEBOOK

TRANSLATED BY DANIEL SLOATE

GUERNICA
TORONTO·BUFFALO·LANCASTER (U.K.)
2001

Original title: *La vie parallèle.*
Copyright © 1994, by André Roy and Les Herbes Rouges.
Translations © 2001, by Daniel Sloate and Guernica Editions Inc.

Antonio D'Alfonso, editor
Guernica Editions Inc.
P.O. Box 117, Station P, Toronto (ON), Canada M5S 2S6
2250 Military Road, Tonawanda, N.Y. 14150-6000 U.S.A.
Gazelle, Falcon House, Queen Square, Lancaster LA1 1RN U.K.

Typeset by Selina.
Printed in Canada.
First edition.

Legal Deposit — Third Quarter
National Library of Canada
Library of Congress Catalog Card Number: 2001095258
National Library of Canada Cataloguing in Publication Data
Roy, André. 1944-
[Vie parallèle. English]
Parallel to life
(Essay series; 45)
Translation of: La vie parallèle.
ISBN 1-55071-143-1
I. Sloate, Daniel. II. Title. III. Title: Vie parallèle. English.
IV. Series: Essays series (Toronto, Ont.) ; 45.
PS8585.O897V5413 2001 C848'.54 C2001-902501-7
PQ3919.2.R65V5313 2001

Contents

Keep a Journal the way one strolls. And strolling could become a spiritual exercise (like poetry for that matter); artful stealing, like a thief, but one's own thoughts in this case.

*

My Journal, a companion to my writings. And will be similar to them: fragments, aphorisms — like my poems.

*

I realize I've almost always kept a journal, but one which could just as easily be scribbled in a notebook or on a piece of paper, or on the back of a book of matches, or on a page in an agenda. What I wrote was words and sentences I had heard and then transformed, seldom a whole poem, usually just a line or two.

*

This is not a Journal, "heavy with the weight of the world," but a notebook of "the unbearable lightness": gratuitous moments, empty moments, bubbles of language, a momentary, and especially non-controlled, flow of words. (Barthes' neologism *bathmology* comes to mind, the interplay of degrees of language which should be the guiding principle of this notebook.)

*

I kept a Journal only once in my life, in 1972, for
three months following a distressful emotional
breakup. The fact is, I'm not interested enough in my
life to keep "tabs" on it.

*

The notebook could be a "treatise on brief marvels"
(the title of a book by the Czech writer Vaclav Jamek,
which he wrote directly in French).

*

The tone of the notebook: immediacy, excitement.
An epiphany (in the Joycean sense). A reflection.
Words collected because I love them. The excitement
in jotting down somewhere a phrase, a reflection.

*

If I ever publish this notebook, I'll have to revise,
change, rework everything — out of respect for the
reader.

*

A note: preparation for a line of poetry. Or: a claim to
life. Or: an excuse for despair.

*

I take notes. I raise my gaze on the world. A notebook
really does allow for thinking freely.

*

A notebook can be a slim volume that says much (about what is in the mind, the heart, the gut).

*

A featherweight notebook (just joking!).

*

No urge to "communicate" with this notebook any more than with my poems.

*

Nonchalant, neglectful when keeping a notebook, but not lazy.

*

A notebook similar to being in a state of watchfulness: ideas flying like phosphenes. (The first time I think I saw the word "phosphene" was in *L'Imaginaire* [The Imaginary] by Jean-Paul Sartre.)

*

"Down with the anecdote!" is the promise I make as I write in these notebooks.

*

Each notebook (generally bought when travelling) where I jot down my notes has a different format.

*

Just a thought, but also a just thought (the underlying principal of the notebook).

*

I have the feeling that keeping this notebook will oblige me to think every day —or nearly.

*

Reach the point, effortlessly, when I can gear my thinking to this notebook.

*

One cigarette, one note (for this notebook). [Author's Note: this entry was written when I was a smoker!]

*

During the time (indefinite) while writing in my notebooks, try and make ideas come more often.

*

I decided to call this book *Daily Notebook* because I write mainly during the day (especially in the morning). The title was inspired by Philippe Sollers' work, *Nocturnal Notebook*.

*

An attempt by means of this notebook to singularize myself and at the same time to keep from unveiling too much of myself. (I could say the same thing as regards my poetry.)

*

Even so, one day try and write a Journal! (Not much difference between Notebooks and Journals, is there?) But write only about the literary aspects and facts of my life.

I still don't know what people read to live.

*

I still don't know what I really gain (or lose) when I write. Has writing changed my personality, for instance? And does my personality make me (better) equipped to write?

*

What I prefer when I read: ambiguity, irony and emotion. (Actually, I look for the same thing in the cinema.)

*

A visit to the Montreal Book Fair: came home exhausted by the mediocre books piled high on the literary landscape. (Do too many books get published? I'm not sure, but there are definitely too many books that are vulgar, in bad taste, badly written, produced by writers of little or no talent.)

*

At the same time at the Fair, not enough money to buy all the books I would like to read.

*

(Not enough time to read all the books I would like to read – should read.)

*

Reading the classics (Châteaubriand at present), an amazing adventure: these authors are audacious and modern; they always surprise, they always dazzle.

*

I do like some comfort and luxury – and I do everything I can to obtain them – if they can safeguard my need to write, an island of solitude, the minimum to survive.

*

True, I seek a certain comfort so I can write: "I have seen so many men of letters who are poor and scorned that I decided long ago I should not increase their number" (Voltaire).

*

November: it's cold already; the right weather to warm oneself up by writing.

*

Yesterday I read a novel (by a Quebecker) about two children: no hint of sexuality. What's the use of continuing? No sex, no style.

*

Our literature, like our cinema, is too discreet, too modest (which is why we have so much trouble getting recognition elsewhere).

*

A young man tells me he is a writer; I feel like saying: "So you're sick, too?"

*

Not enough blue in the sky today for me to write. As lazy as light?

*

Sometimes in despair when the feeling comes over me that I'm condemned to solitude because I'm a writer. And yet how well I know that my solitude is the sole possession I can call my own as a writer.

*

I don't want to have a beautiful style, I want to have *my* style. (A beautiful style soon becomes affected, formal and boring.)

*

Style, above all, is a matter of structure, order, and taste.

*

Style: a vision of the world – an irreplaceable one.

*

Give the impression my poetry is simple and "accessible," as we say.

*

I'm trying in French to find my Quebeckness. (Where would my Quebeco-Americanicity be situated?)

*

Everything I write is close to me without being anecdotal.

*

I don't think I have kept anything from my travels for my books.

*

What is it in me that makes me a poet?

*

My poems must surprise me before anything else. I tell myself they will then surprise the reader. Excitement on both sides.

*

I write poetry. Yes, I do. I allow myself to do so because the world is full of poems that have not been written.

*

I don't react much to prestige and the public. The fact I continue to write poetry rather than starting a novel is proof enough I think.

*

Dogged by melancholy. Regrets, occasionally, about not being read enough. And some, very rare, about not being recognized by the university establishment.

*

My life in my words, probably the only life that can explain my life as a whole.

*

The writer finds sense in the core of all things. (As I was writing this, I typed "gore" instead of "core." Ah, those *lapsi!*)

*

Writing has always seemed to me to be a good reason for living.

*

The only time I'm afraid of myself is when I write.

*

Be courageous enough to write.

*

The occupation of a saint. What is? Writing!

*

Writers: penitents. Gifted for grief.

*

A writer: modest, aware, anxiety-ridden as well as proud, meditative, strong-minded.

*

I'm quoting from memory a phrase I'm fond of by Arthur Miller: "The writer's job is to give the impression he knows much more than he really does."

THE BEST VICE OF ALL: READING

Reading slowly is a real exercise in knowledge. No bulimia, no fat: the bright, meticulous path. Reading with persistence, close to writing in that respect.

*

Reading and thinking: true literature demands these two functions — simultaneously.

*

"The pleasure of the text," yes, indeed!

*

A work of art exists only when there is a blend of intention and attention, as Gérard Genette says.

*

Remove ourselves from the chaos of the world and our era through books.

*

Great books are books that lend themselves to endless interpretation.

*

For the writer, the reader is like his fraternal twin.

*

Books: offerings or sufferings?

*

Joyful despair in books . . .

*

The reader should not reduce himself to seeking a single meaning or a single interpretation. Reading is a gathering, an effort, it's astonishment.

*

At the surface of words (radiance, mirror, reflections), the core of things.

*

It's reading, not writing, that casts a net over words and gives meaning to a text.

*

Reading is tension between the author and the reader; the I is ubiquitous, and yet the reader is autonomous. A tug of love-war between the two of us.

*

A book always tells the truth if it is *written*.

*

Writing is to weave a web around the void we find ourselves in, as Jean Claude Pirotte says. Reading is to fill the void (readers are our salvation)

*

Tears and pain nourish words. Books therefore become the place where unrestricted thought reveals all our dignity, all our moral sense, because they translate the individual expression of our collective sufferings.

*

I can state unequivocally that reading and writing are freedom.

*

The freedom of discovering oneself through books, an inestimable and unique means of knowledge. (Unacceptable, say the powers that be. What about schools, education, newspapers, television? Power structures are against freedom.)

*

We can learn more in one book than in twelve years of school. Proof that we can learn only by ourselves.

*

The aim of books is to treat all that lives like a soul, which is the opposite of audiovisual technology. It treats humans like a motor, an inanimate being that needs excitement, hyper sensations to enable the image of a human to be drawn (the illusion expanded). (I'm reading Paul Virilio.)

*

Each book projects a new and different lighting on the world.

*

Reading: a certain form of debauchery, perversion! An unpunished vice, as Valéry Larbaud says. Taking advantage of books: how marvellous!

LIVE TO WRITE AND WRITE TO LIVE

One has to write in the knowledge that writing is harmful to society (to society, not to the world).

*

Born to take everything as grist for writing, I'm not sure about. Live to take everything as grist for writing, I'm sure about.

*

The fact one writes cannot be explained – and never will be.

*

Always thinking about writing. Maybe this explains my near-chronic fatigue.

*

Live long to write long.

*

Try to be in a permanent creative state. But in that case one would have to be in a constant state of exaltation.

*

Eternity is present when one writes.

*

Writing is an antidote – temporary and ephemeral – for despair.

*

Anyone who has failed in his attempts at writing wants to be reasonable (he's ready to start over again), whereas anyone who has failed in love doesn't want to be (love is forever).

*

The act of writing: pain and celebration.

*

Also: the act of writing is pleasure and martyrdom.

*

Writing is a way of life.

*

It also means living a thousand contradictions.

*

Writing is like plunging into the unknown and will find its egress in that which I know not.

*

Writing books seems to me to be a little less foolish way of wasting my time.

*

Decide to write to change things, knowing full well changing things is hopeless.

*

Pledge yourself to one necessity only: writing.

*

When I write I can say I am still alive. Write to see whether I exist.

*

Writing: a good step stolen on life!

POETRY IS A FORM

Despite what one thinks, a poem has no centre of gravity, no hard core. Its cohesion comes from elsewhere, from an interplay of particles called lines, which are clusters of sparks and arrows that come together as we finish reading the poem to form a totality. The totality is the book.

*

A few words are enough to give a poem its tone, but it's the way they collide and interact, often quite violently (because their interplay is as unexpected as it is marvellous), that they reveal the subject, the substance, the core.

*

It's better not to approach my poems head on, but to go around them because they are never closed upon themselves. It's better to enter by the side door.

*

No transparent, unified or linear discourse, but lines like fragments breaking the flow of the text as one reads. These breaks, like leaps, interrupt the poem and set up a new writing, a new poetic order that allows the reader to grasp the meaning *in another way.*

*

My poems are really a tug of war between form and substance. This is why I don't believe my poems are lost or empty as was trumpeted in the 1960s when formalism held sway, and the cult of poetry for poetry's sake. Words don't duplicate reality; they don't transcribe it just the way it is: they juxtapose the reality produced by the poem with "real" reality. The poem sets up a relationship – of struggle or complementarity – with the real. Between the poem and the real – similar to the relationship between form and substance – there is permanent query.

*

When the real enters a poem, it sets up a conflict, a tension between the lines, between the words; meaning is established through this conflict and tension.

*

Poetry is a form – like everything we cherish in a human being: eyes, face, hands. And I love this form. Today I find ridiculous the accusation by critics (which I think stemmed at the time from a narrow view of literature) that castigated us poets of *Les Herbes rouges* and *La Barre du jour* generation as "formalists." I laugh at their criticism maintaining we preferred form over substance (which, of course, they looked upon as solely a solipsistic and conceited choice). And yet one has only to read the great writers (Mallarmé, Proust, Joyce, Artaud, to name a few) to realize what the *violence* of form is all about. Experiencing this violence, which was like an echo of the violence in my daily life, I'm sure I started to write because I very quickly realized it had substance.

*

Poetry cannot continue unless it can still modify our perspective on the world (the better to see it).

*

Poetry will perish when it isn't the esthetic experience of perception anymore. Poetry will perish when it turns into a consumer product (which is what some want to do to poetry, in the same way they've done to the novel).

*

Poetry must remain, for anyone who chooses to write it, a *terra incognita* where everything is still to be written.

*

Poetry: awareness. Poetry: thought. Foundation of creation, of writing.

*

The ever-growing certitude of knowing nothing about poetry when I write a poem — and even when I'm not writing!

*

Show poetry's workings in the poem. All those words that are nothing but an eternal pursuit in order to render reality . . . Their follow-up is the present work.

*

Poetry is rhythm. Lines, breaks, repetitions exist to render the rhythm perceptible.

*

"Subvert" form. The movement to subvert form, as they said in the 1970s, was often looked upon by those who judged and condemned us, as an expression of scorn for the reader. Whereas it was only a means – one of the means, but we had adopted specifically that one – to stimulate the reader, to persuade him (persuade him that we were worth his affection?). A real tug of war, like a love relationship! We were telling the reader in this way that reading is not to be confused with an act of banality, routine and digestible; reading is a research, we were saying, a query, a violent appropriation (like theft) of the text and its meanings; nothing is given, but all is to be taken (as in love!).

*

The subversion of form, disputing it, pulverizing it, so misunderstood by the critics, was after all just another way of creating poetry. Each decade has its own way!

*

A poetry laboratory to discover a language of poetry. An exact science (the novel would be classified as an applied science).

*

I'm thinking of a Poetry that becomes greater than all the different kinds of poetry, greater than all the different forms of poetry!

*

Form is my obsession. Maybe my only obsession!

*

Poetry: a new language that one has to learn all over again all the time. (Language: object of love, of knowledge.)

*

The language of poetry is a language of pleasure.

*

When I write, I never feel the urge to communicate. Poetry rejects the tyranny of information since, in its essence, poetry is ineffectual analytically and descriptively. It projects us into that dangerous realm known as the unreadable, the "unenunciable," the unutterable.

*

Poetry is research because it can never put a final period to writing.

*

Writing poetry is to reach the point where the meaning of words vanishes and leaves poetry in its stead.

*

Writing poetry is to create forms so that through my writing one can see the world in a different way. (Quite a claim!)

*

Other writings (poetry since Villon, let's say): a repertoire that is useful to me. I can situate myself in terms of them, I mean I can bring them to me, make them mine (I can quote them, plagiarize them, delete them, transform them and invent my very own writing). They open up the horizon for me and encourage me more than ever to be suspicious of any imposed form; the authors of these writings have experienced, over the course of the years, every risk, given in to every temptation and by so doing have renewed their writings. I want to be different from other poets, but identified with the movement of universal writing they belong to and which makes poetry unfinished, "unfinishable," interminable.

*

Poetry as a parallel life, better, more exciting, and more pertinent also, more "moral." Like a great shadow cast over me, a protection, a call, an obligation, an adventure. At the street corner: poetry. That's what keeps me going on my way.

WRITING IS AN ALTERNATIVE

Writing as a means to reaching the real.

*

Writing forges our resistance to "social well-being."

*

Writing inevitably condemns us to the fringe, to ex-
ile: it's to be torn between solitude and surrendering
ourselves to society, to its notorious promise of social
well-being.

*

Writing: a battle waged against society in order to be
with the world.

*

Writing must not submit to any authority – or else
disappear.

*

Writing does not allow us to entertain any nostalgia
or regrets.

*

Writing comes from an elsewhere I do not know,
which I will never know. I write because I do not
know where I come from.

*

Writing is the opposite of language: it moves, is never the same, is innumerable, always paradoxical, oblivious; it is a thousand forms, amoral, it is rejection of language, of all languages, unqualifiable.

*

We can always learn from our breathing, our voice, our writing.

*

Writing connects me to the solitude of others, to the solitude of writers, to all the solitudes that help me find mine.

*

Speech plays with alternates (there are always possibilities); writing is an alternative only (with writing one can proceed only toward the impossible).

*

No rules, no laws in writing; nothing but vast, insolent freedom.

*

Revealing the cipher of the world's mystery is the role that could be assigned to writing. (Read Mallarmé again.)

*

Look upon writing occasionally as a battle waged against oneself, against one's faults, one's mediocrity.

*

Writing is always a comparison: it *situates* you.

*

Writing makes one untamable.

*

Everything that underlies writing: the unconscious, namely fantasies, instincts, drives . . . (Everything that is sexual.)

*

In writing, the adventure of the world and the adventure of language blend inextricably together.

*

After a certain number of years writing, after reaching a certain level in the course of one's life, it's no longer life that forces itself on writing but writing that forces itself on life.

*

Indebted to writing, I always feel obliged to finish a book.

*

Integrate one's love of literature into a strategy of writing.

*

Writing makes me different from others, whereas ever since my birth, death, who will come to meet me one day, has made me the same as others. Death simply makes me share in the common destiny of man.

NEW ATTEMPTS AT KEEPING A
JOURNAL

Don't forget that my latest poems were written during the siege of Sarajevo and Gorazde in Yugoslavia.

*

Vocabulary too inadequate and poor to express my horror, my pain and my helplessness at what is happening in Yugoslavia.

*

What can I do against the war in ex-Yugoslavia? Continue writing . . .

*

Life goes on. There is war and then there will be peace, like sunshine after rain. Life goes on. Writing commands me to continue living with life.

*

Surprise and bitterness, innocence and consternation, gaiety and sadness, patience and rebellion against the facts and events falling across my desire to write.

*

Listening to the recent song by Rita Mitsouko about hate, I say to myself, yes, indeed, there is not only love in books, but hate as well. Write against all those who perpetrate massacres anywhere, torture and rape.

*

I want to write poems that are sharp, red-hot, dramatic, close to Time and History, the grief that explodes in life and the conflicts that run through it.

*

Poetry and thought, for me, should always coincide. (This note should please François Charron.)

*

I like each line of a poem to impress like evidence, to be in itself an idea that is unique, singular, extraordinary.

*

When I write I never, ever have the impression that what I'm doing is a social act.

*

My impalpable difference due to my writing.

*

The shadow of doubt that falls on me whenever I write . . . Tremblings . . . Later, when night comes, anguish overcomes me . . .

*

Pleased to have finished an article with the following statement: "A work condemned by the formal void that is draining it."

*

The travels I've been on, I've never done them since I've never written a word about them!

*

The flesh is not sad, and I've not read every book since I still have several to write.

*

An editor states he receives collections of poems and complains that their authors don't include any instructions. Well no, there simply is no single set of instructions about how to read poetry. These are forged by oneself, book after book – especially since every book contains its own instructions that have to be discovered. A little more effort is required, Mr. Editor, where poetry is concerned!

*

Even before he reads a collection of poems, the same editor is overcome with a touch of boredom. A little more effort is required, Mr. Editor, where oneself is concerned!

*

I have an inquisitive mind, I'm always in a hurry to read a new collection of poems, a new author. Unfortunately, four books out of five slip from my fingers. And yet I do make an effort . . .

*

Alberto Minguel, born in Argentina, is a francophone writer who lives here and who has just published with Seuil *Dernières Nouvelles d'une terre abandonnée* (what a beautiful title!) [*Latest News from an Abandoned Land.*] He says Quebec is a country that allows him, in the realm of the imaginary, to collaborate on its definition and which gives him a feeling of civic euphoria. What about us Quebeckers, what about us Quebecois writers, are we curious about our country? What language should we use to get to know it?

*

Language is a basic thing for a country, a culture; language, that essential thing for writers, must become *the* true language, a living and varied entity; it must be the true value.

*

Much information in the world of today; many pious sentiments pouring from radio and television; increase in clichés as reviews and magazines proliferate. Desperately few thoughts, little sensitivity or imagination. Here is the main reason for the primordial importance of reading over any other activity.

*

Mass media: no memory, much forgetting. A book, a real book, always leaves an internal scar.

*

I suddenly remembered with a little pang the literary life of the 1970s, the launchings, twice a week at the Éditions du Jour, the impromptu meetings. An ambience which, in retrospect, seems benevolent and friendly, and which has vanished — regrettably, because it was a cultural stimulus. Literature, which is reading and publication as much as it is spiritual activity, has become a private phenomenon (and by "private" I don't mean solitary).

POETRY WILL NOT PERISH

Poets I have read this season (I'm arranging their books in my library): Yehuda Amichaï, Claude Beausoleil, Christian Bobin, Denise Boucher, Daniel Boulanger, Michel Calonne, William Cliff, Philippe Delaveau, René Depestre, Gunnar Ekelöf, Werner Lambersy, Michael Palmer, Pierre de Ronsard, Martin-Pierre Tremblay.

*

Poetry was the first literary form (*The Odyssey*): it still is the most modern of forms.

*

Poetry: not frozen words, but images released by words and which will travel through time and space.

*

Poetry makes space its breath, its research, its material.

*

To write poetry, there has to be immense sensitivity, fine intelligence, a dash of obliviousness – and the insane atoms of the air at the terrible five o'clocks in the afternoon.

*

Poets, vagabonds also (novelists are like travelling salesmen next to them).

*

A book of poems has just been published: an event as incredible and unexpected as the birth of a star so distant its existence won't be known for millions of light-years to come. Patience in poetry's azure realm!

*

Poetry: words, the concrete matter of language, writing you can touch.

*

Writing poetry for me amounts to never bowing to the dictates of language and letters. Always challenging clichés, codes, rules.

*

The poet as the purest type of man, as Hermann Hesse says.

*

Poetry: vertigo revealed.

*

The lament of the world's worst things can be heard in poetry.

*

Writing a book of poems is fine; I won't be able to put everything into it. Its composition involves tension, requires constant surveillance, takes stock of my sensitivity and my knowledge. I have to be both logical and flexible, accurate and ambiguous. I have to work at the writing machine (machination!) and lose myself in my task. Must be timid but ambitious, present but ephemeral, intelligent but "unattainable," difficult but moving, must succeed but not accept.

*

Poets: canvassers of the infinite.

*

The poem: the voice of voices.

*

The words in poetry: adults.

*

The poem where silence breaks into words like a thief.

*

A way of writing worse than terrible: writing poetry.

*

Every day in the poem is like a last day.

*

In the poem, it is compulsory to live writing physically, materially, concretely.

*

The unreconciled. Who are? Poets!

*

Poets: marginals of marginals.

*

Writing poetry is true folly. Something inexplicable, obscure, like the words and gestures of a madman.

*

Poetry will not perish! (Repeat a hundred times, a thousand times: "Poetry will not perish!")

THE WRITER WRITES FOR ALL

I am well aware that sometimes people reproach me for being too gay, in other words for not being universal enough, or only slightly universal, too marginal or too "subculture" (allusion to the homosexual subculture). The same old political and chauvinistic refrain that keeps coming back, will always come back, and is loud and clear in the so proper present climate of the times. (Is this why I'm invited so seldom to conferences, conventions, and institutions of learning?)

*

I don't write for a specialized public; I'm writing for everyone. (But who will believe me?)

*

I don't ask my readers to become homosexuals as they read my work. But I do want, or rather I demand that they enter into my writing, and accept it momentarily, even if they reject it afterwards. I ask them to lose themselves as they read, dissolve as they read, lose control of themselves! My writing will *succeed* if that happens.

*

Neither saint nor martyr when I write. Not even gay!

*

By the singularity of my writing I must unnerve people. Gently unnerve them. A book is such a sign of
love!

*

Love? Of course! Write and divide.

*

A constraint then, when I write, to never make con-
cessions.

*

A wish to remain gentle when I write. (Don't I ma-
nipulate the reader by my gentleness?)

*

Wish for gentleness but attain it through a certain
aggressiveness (directed against myself). So remain
gently aggressive when I write . . .

*

When I write I don't let myself go; I might even say
I never let myself go. The moments I spend writing
is the only time I don't flinch, when I am *stiff*, ready
and bristling, ready for any danger — the dangers I
have created myself!

*

The material I draw my poems from may be trivial,
vile, but the poems themselves must always be noble
and lofty, above all ordinary values. (What I just said

can be stated differently: take what is not approved of and make it acceptable through writing.)

*

Avoid feeling doomed because I'm a homosexual, but because I'm a writer.

*

Homosexual: minority. Writer: minority. Minority in a minority!

*

I substitute the rules of esthetics for the rules of social morality.

*

I write to escape insignificance (of habits and daily deeds) and come back to the essential (which, therefore, must have been lost, right?).

*

I don't think any feelings of guilt can be found in my texts.

*

I often feel, as I write, that I have exceeded my limits because I overcome challenges and accomplish important feats in my texts. I'm always surprised, after a session, to have written. I'm in control of myself and yet I'm not sure of anything in what I write. Dreadful, merciless.

*

Constantly overcome by doubts as to the quality and value of my texts. (This is something the reader must never sense.)

*

Constantly torn between the desire to write only poetry and a wish to intervene in the debates of society — a wish that is somewhat fulfilled, but often not enough, by my work as a critic. I have noticed, by the way, that few writers are critics, particularly in the weekly literary sections of the newspapers. Why are our writers not committed to any great extent? It's true that the directors of the media are very suspicious of them.

*

Nothing I want to write is easy. But I don't want that to ever be apparent.

*

Writing means you have to be patient.

*

The writer is a thief of the words of others so he can return them to others.

All is written when I write.

*

No writing without solitude. I write alone, but also with all writers.

*

My doubts contain my solitude as a writer.

*

As a writer I enjoy the privilege of being able to stick my nose into everything.

*

No subjects in my books: writing only – which I want to be as bare as possible.

*

It may be true that some books are difficult, that one needs a certain background (studies, books) in order to read them. This is a mere detail. (But *they*, the media people, pounce on this to try and make the public see a flaw. But this is not a flaw!)

*

At times, the terror of writing.

*

I know that disaster is part of writing.

*

I have a feeling my words are not always up to the task of relating the disaster (one's own or the disasters of others).

*

Always try and go beyond the act of writing; I mean try and go deeper and deeper into writing itself.

*

Writing: lots of work, doubts, gropings, daydreams, availability . . .

*

In spite of everything, one must have great confidence in oneself to write.

*

When I write, I know I am in the company of other and greater writers than I. And yet this fact is not distressing to me.

*

At times, writing to the point of tears, to total exhaustion. As Duras says: up to the point of one's own disappearance (she was describing the death of a fly). All the energy spent in writing stuns me completely.

*

I don't want my books to be like anything else.

*

I've often noticed I can't talk to anyone – not even another writer – about the book I happen to be working on. Maybe talking about it would ruin it . . . Always doomed to be alone with my book.

*

I admit I protect myself a lot when I write: I'm careful to avoid problems (no falling in love when I start on a new project), I'm careful about my health, etc. All this in an effort to save my book from the possibility of loss.

*

Marguerite Duras states in Benoît Jacquot's film *Écrire* [Writing] that one writes so as not to commit suicide. Exactly so! I can't imagine what I would do if the purpose of my life were not writing and if I didn't have the chance to do so. I repeat: writing *saves* me.

*

Writing helps me to be what I am.

*

I don't mind the notion of writing for another, even though I don't expect a great deal from him. But I also know that without him I wouldn't be a writer.

*

I have the impression I made a vow to withdraw from society when I decided quite young, around eighteen, to devote myself to the writer's life, which replaced the priesthood I was destined for.

NOT ALL THE BOOKS HAVE BEEN
WRITTEN YET

Over-indulging in literature – the way we speak of over-indulgence at table. It makes us ill, an over-indulgence in living.

*

Reading to be able to live since reading is already living intensely. Yes, reading is a way of living.

*

Books really contain something that is more than life.

*

The great joy that books procure for us in our discovery of new authors . . .

*

One advantage of reading is meeting friends who have often been dead for a very long time.

*

Reading a book: an exceptional moment in one's life.

*

Books are a quest for signs, symbols, traces of the irreducible experience that life is.

*

A book can be a thing of terror for the reader since it calls his whole being into question. And since it is confrontation, there can be no consolation.

*

Books offer that which cannot be found anywhere else, in life, that is: a call to what is beyond, what is over and above life.

*

Books are elsewhere, but an elsewhere which is right here with me (and it has nothing to do with exoticism).

*

Humanity takes on its name again in books.

*

Any book steeped in knowledge becomes the heir to that knowledge; this is the result of modernism.

*

A book is not worthless because it is successful.

*

It has been said that all books have been written and . . . Not true! Not at all!

*

In great books, one can always find these three elements: sex, money, and death.

*

Books always wear masks; they provide an approach that is more sensitive, more cruel and more painful than reality.

*

Books can be a way to display one's despair but with courtesy, elegance, and a dash of perversity.

*

A wish for books to reach the non-reader. Actually, the latter is the true public (the paradox here is in appearance only).

*

In books I meet a counter-society (read *Remembrance of Things Past* to grasp my affirmation).

*

Books rid us of our guilt: we find stories that don't conform to society's ideals.

*

Reading gives us the opportunity to observe human nature up close.

*

Books are a declaration of faith made by an unbeliever, Bibles written by the Devil.

*

Reading is a passion, but it can also be a profession, an exceptional one at that, since it not only makes us think but dream as well.

*

Reading: a double life.

I write poetry because I feel I am better equipped now, especially after more than twenty years of practice (and to stop would be insane) at crystallizing emotions.

*

Enter poetry the way one enters religion, but without hope (of finding oneself, of finding God).

*

What rebellious force drove me to adopt poetry as a life line, a writing line?

*

I don't believe my poetry — or any other form of writing — can be of help socially — for gays, let's say. And in any case, there are unions, coalitions, militants who will do more than I could ever do.

*

My works won't change the world. I do hope though that they change the way we look at it.

*

I want my poetry to shock the spirit of the church, the police, scientists, priests, and the dissection amphitheatre, as Antonin Artaud wrote to Jacques Prevel.

*

Poetry: the language of the abandoned, the discon-
nected, the persecuted.

*

Poetry: the language, when all is said and done, that
has succeeded.

*

Poems are an essential text. When writing a poem,
one has to be aware of the essential text we all carry
inside us.

*

Going perpetually beyond, that's what poetry is.

*

Poetry: a laboratory of esthetics, a laboratory of
thought.

*

James Sacré reflects that what moves him in poetry is
perhaps an attempt on his part to measure and assimi-
late the territory of a certain love where poetry is the
Other's language.

*

What an inestimable opportunity it is to become familiar with the mysterious adventures of poetry.

*

Poetry is an experiment. It results in feelings, emotions. A curious process involving the transformation of matter.

*

Paul Éluard, in *L'Amour, la poésie* [Love, Poetry], calls poets watchers of grief. A good definition of the poet.

*

Rabelais, in *Le Tiers Livre* [Book Three], states that when poets are near death they usually become prophets.

THE SCRIBE'S WAGES

I think another reason one writes is because there are
accounts to settle – with oneself, one's family, with
society.

*

Writing is to explore one thing only: oneself. Therefore writing about oneself becomes a duty.

*

A writer never stops writing about himself, about
childhood, unforgettable wounds, never stops exercis-
ing his memory, his experiences (this task is more
concrete than one might think).

*

Writing is accompanied by a long and interminable
investigation of mourning; one must realize this and
be conscious of it each and every day.

*

If a book amazes, its author must have been amazed
before us.

*

Taking a book by its form is to lead us into the world
and its secrets.

*

The writer: he who gives the latest news about mankind. His duty: to destroy all consensus of opinion.

*

Writing sets off alarm bells.

*

A perfect ruffian: another good definition of the writer.

*

Maybe because everything is yet to be said that writers still exist.

*

Dancing on the edge of a precipice is a good definition of a writer's function.

*

One "enters" literature alone so as to meet others, the Other.

*

Everything exists for the writer as long as he can write about it, but it is a challenge to his language. The writer can do nothing but confront it since he is the privileged chosen one. No discourse can affect its irreducible nature.

*

Writing constantly calls the writer into question, challenges his social identity; his presence is a denial of social discourse itself. (But the world could cast doubt on writing if it could ever impose the idea of the writer's defeat through the very act of writing.)

*

He provides very few services for his fellow men. Who's that? The writer of course.

*

The writer can only feel indignation at his human predicament – at the predicament we all find ourselves in.

*

A writer gets up every morning refusing to accept the world as it is. Writing is to combat the insufferable moral and spiritual misery of life, the general breakdown in values which blurs our vision of reality.

*

Writers are guided by a desire to be clairvoyant.

*

Writing confirms the fact it is a need which will never be satisfied once we are in thrall to it.

*

The writer's work must be situated outside the social framework (I'm thinking here of the literary establishment and the reading public). This work alone justifies his life.

*

Writing means acknowledging a debt towards other writers.

*

Are writing and happiness incompatible? If a writer is happy, he is a curious exception. Writers have a tendency to subscribe to misfortune.

*

A whole life of freedom . . . that's what a writer's life is.

*

The written page: the writer's wages.

*

A writer has not even an economic status, so how could he have a social status?

*

The real question: one writes to be loved. The real answer: one is a writer when one is loved.

*

A writer crystallizes many forms of hatred around himself (think in this respect of the literary milieu and the world of the university).

*

Ambitious humility of the writer. Humble ambition of the writer.

*

The writer's moral: ambiguity.

*

Writers are those who don't speak the same language as other people. One might say that modernism was born when it was decided not to speak like others, when it was understood that writing is born of language – the writer's, even if it means it is not understood by all. This is the fundamental and intractable law of modernism, and every book must be measured by the spirit of this law.

*

The act of writing for every writer commands him to go to the limits of himself. Life is unbearable for any writer who does not obey this commandment.

*

A duty to write. A duty to read.

*

Write for others who can't express themselves through writing.

*

Writer, *writor* (Barthes), *scribe* (Louis René des Forêts).

*

For des Forêts, the scribe is a writer in thrall to a "mysterious force." Let's expand this remark by saying the scribe is someone who writes constantly, obsessively, a madman who works endlessly, exhaustively, who ferociously tracks down the fleeting word, the "chatterbox" (the title of a novel by des Forêts) awaiting ultimate silence – the person who, in spite of himself, is forced to write.

*

Stubbornly writing – what a singular phenomenon! Even the prospect of failure or silence can't stop it.

*

Every writer has experienced the temptation of silence at least once: perhaps one time or several times in a day, one day or several days in his life. Some mysterious force prevents his succumbing. In any case, only death can impose silence on the writer.

*

The writer wishes to remain alive for others and dead to society.

FINAL ATTEMPTS AT KEEPING A JOURNAL

I like knowing that Jean Genet never used the word "writer" to describe himself; he always called himself a "poet."

*

Ultimately, it's the adversary of society in me who is honoured whenever I'm encouraged, or given prizes.

*

One always comes back to the notion of freedom: writing must have no fetters and yet is fettered to freedom.

*

I desire the world and I am disappointed by the world. My writings are rooted in this contradiction.

*

I'm more interested in the human condition in general than in individuals in particular. This is why people say (scornfully? ironically?) that I write poetry.

*

The impression that everything I do will one day serve to nourish my writings.

*

Justify one's life through writing. I'm trying, I'm trying.

*

Writing is a way for me to give life to my emotions; I give them free rein in my texts.

*

My life would be impossible to live if I couldn't use it in my writing. People don't realize that by so doing I make my life possible.

*

I am at the school for feelings when I write. I want each book to open up on the emotions.

*

Find a style, the style that is directly opposed to the vulgarity and bleakness of everyday language, that language which can never be transcribed into books unless all notion of writing is to disappear. Each word must be selected in terms of the other words in order to take its rightful place in the line; once there, the word is unshakably permanent since it has been rele-gated to that place only, and is there as though it had always been in that particular place. Get to the point where I can say to myself that words selected by the writer can only be those he has written, and that no other word can be substituted for it in the context of the poem. As though the word I've chosen is unique.

*

Expect one day to be accused of being a thief of words.

*

The text is my unending dream.

*

A text that is resistant to me is a text I need.

*

A definite impression that writing has physically cured me after my youthful years when I was sick so often, and that writing is the reason I've been in fairly good health for thirty years if one doesn't include, as a friend said ironically, my opportunistic illnesses like colds, ulcers, the flu, etc.

*

No serious illnesses or accidents so far. Writing has protected me!

*

Luckily one doesn't have to understand everything (the world, people, their actions) to start writing.

*

Remain faithful to myself and continue to amaze myself at the same time.

*

In Peter Handke's book, *Images du recommencement* [Images from Starting Over], the author speaks of rediscovering the words of his childhood. Mine were English words (*plug*, *switch*, *shed*). Problem: how to write my quebeckness in French?

*

Writing almost always raises my spirits. Writing cannot fail to raise one's spirits, right?

*

I've written a lot. Over six hundred pages this year: reviews, poems, a notebook, the beginnings of a book on the cinema. Almost no one knows this (who is interested in my career?). The years pass. Work a lot so I won't die an idiot. And who cares what people think of me? Just have the courage to write. I've found such joy in writing and an excellent reason for living. Expect nothing. Above all, don't complain. (André, stop it right now!)

ON COMMITMENT

I don't know if it's because I live in Quebec but I often have the impression when I write (and the feeling reaches its paroxysm especially when one of my books is published) that I'm putting up resistance to the death of something called art, or at other times something called culture, or language, or literature. Maybe this is the true commitment of a writer, i.e., resistance.

*

When a writer thinks his works are misunderstood, or even useless, he might give in to the temptation to commit himself to some political movement; when the writer is successful, when astronomical quantities of his books are sold and when he thinks he can influence social or political trends, he might decide to become committed. Neither one of these reasons is valid, nor do they make him qualified, through his commitment to a cause, to immerse himself in social or political issues.

*

If a writer becomes committed to a cause, it's because he doesn't believe in the efficacy of literature. Some people will say: "With good reason!"

*

Gorki, Hamson, Pirandello, Pound: don't forget these writers, along with many others, for their question-able, unspeakable or reprehensible commitments.

*

Before joining a party or a movement, think of writ-ing — and the pleasure it affords one. (Down with masochism!)

*

If there is commitment by reason of force or from duty, or because of ethical and moral motives, maybe one should resign oneself to the fact knowing that a price will have to be paid.

*

Mixing politics and literature is no easy task.

*

But is it enough to commit oneself because one is morally certain of a cause? It's always possible to make a mistake.

*

We must also realize we are all responsible, in varying degrees of course, for what happens or might happen to our country, especially when threats of tyranny loom on the political horizon (I'm thinking in this instance of the present situation in Italy, where a post-fascist movement has appeared). Feel responsible, but not guilty!

*

Keep in mind the fact that writing already rejects what is happening. So . . .

*

If you're a bad writer, you'll probably make a bad politician.

*

One can be committed by continuing to write: by writing critical reviews, for instance, because it is an excellent means to make one's ideas known.

*

Should a writer commit himself to a cause because no definite answer will ever be given to his questions? Can a writer commit himself through despair because he is devoured by a pessimistic view of life that makes him profoundly unhappy and incapable of writing? Yes, but the risk of making a deeply serious mistake is very real.

*

Commitment, or the (good?) use of pessimism. (In this respect, I could write a treatise here in praise of nihilism.)

*

Before undertaking any action, be aware of the eternity of every second in the written text.

*

It's imperative to establish a moral point of reference for men and women (the writer does exactly this) and not so much an increase in the standard of living (politicians do this to the detriment of the former).

*

Committing oneself to a cause because one has nothing more to lose is a bad reason — one more to add to the list!

*

Keen lucidity will invariably put an end to political commitment.

*

If one is to take on a commitment to something, one has to believe in life. Every book is written to combat this futile faith.

*

Commitment can be a tool for combatting anxiety. And solitude also. So? It's an easy solution and self-delusion.

*

People commit themselves to a cause because they feel unworthy to belong to the circle of the masters of disenchantment, namely writers, artists, creators.

*

You can't see the writer as a convert.

*

Politicians cannot abide poets. Poetry serves no ideology and can only piss off politicians.

*

Politicians are generally bibliophobic. In this respect, I remember an interview with Claude Ryan published in *L'Actualité* wherein he stated he was pleased with himself for never having read even one novel since he finished school: he was the minister of education at the time! The unflagging mediocrity of politicians!

*

Writers must always put forth their claim to their fundamental uselessness.

*

Literature is, and must always remain, unacceptable.

Even a macabre poem can be beautiful if it is true. A poem about misery can make us happy.

*

My poetry is a collage in which I try to establish a correspondence between disparate elements, and to make unexpected associations appear natural.

*

The vocabulary I use in my books is lean; I have always used simple words to avoid closing poetry in upon itself – and this was true even at the height of the formalist movement. Actually, the real question is whether my gamble paid off. And the answer cannot come from me.

*

When I write, I always try to be surprised at the act of writing poetry.

*

When speaking of a reality which does not affect me physically – AIDS, for instance, which was the case when I wrote *On sait que cela a été écrit avant et après la grande maladie* [We know that this was written before and after the great scourge] – I used *my* words and made the reality of AIDS my reality.

*

Remember that the so-called "I," whether social or mental, is not reflected in the poem. To write about the "I" is more like an attempt to destroy it.

*

Poetry is an inner experience of language. The only way I have to make the world mine is through language.

*

"Poetic poetry is a void in the torn fabric of the world of men" wrote the German romantic poet Ernst Meister (1911-1979). I could add to his remark: ". . . and in the torn fabric of the world of words."

*

The poetry of poetry.

*

Poetry's truth is not concealed in Reason's realm.

*

Whenever I write a poem, I'm always tempted to push everything to extreme limits.

*

It is thanks to the way I set up my life style and not due to my books that I have been a writer for more than twenty years. Even a long practice of writing is of little help with a new book. In fact, it sometimes seems to be a burden.

*

I can also assert that each new book is an attempt to liberate both me as a person, and the latest book from the preceding ones.

*

I can also assert that every book is a fresh version of reality added to the preceding versions, completing them as it dismantles them.

PORTRAIT OF THE WRITER

The writer is someone who does not look upon misery as normal – or upon happiness, love, or life in general for that matter, as normal. He can draw from this truth a marvellous book, joyful and luminous. He can make a reader happy about Evil for a few hours.

*

Anguish, which ultimately is what makes us write, is neither interesting or pleasurable for the writer but paradoxically the despair in what he writes, is.

*

Peter Handke made the observation that each writer bars the way to other writers so they can find their own way.

*

Write to get to know the other, certainly, but to know oneself as well. A sharing of otherness.

*

One's sexual condition (not orientation!) is what makes one write. Writing is an experience which opens the way to pleasure.

*

One writes with one's penis.

*

Write because there is no one left to conquer but oneself.

*

Write to set down a moral code still concealed from
oneself.

*

Patience is the great virtue of the writer. Why hurry
when he has all eternity before him?

*

Writing means to progress but only in the void.

*

To write is to dare.

*

The writer: the companion, the researcher, the unrav-
eller.

*

The writer: a front row spectator.

*

Or again: the writer is a developer (like the liquid
used in photography).

*

Or yet again: a disturbing and dangerous guy.

*

The singular aspect of a writer is his having written. His life means something to me if he has lived *differently* (if he has striven to be an *other*).

*

The writer draws new maps of a territory, from points both inside and out, blurs borders, undermines systems, sows disorder, disorganizes nature and society, destroys identities and connections between them, makes the familiar strange, dislocates language.

*

The writer's intuition is similar to a scientist's research but not necessarily with any knowledge of it.

*

In the name of sociability and the freedom of information as one's right, people want to know everything about a writer and his private life. Usually this results in nothing more than untruths or one-dimensional truths, skewed and vulgar.

*

The writer springs from an experience that is unsuspectable, unassimilatable, and inconceivable that his books hint at but do not reveal; they conceal this experience by lifting the veil on a part of it and they protect it by fleeing from it.

*

No one can say with total exactitude why this particular writer wrote that particular book.

*

What sort of life was the writer leading when he wrote such and such a book? Why the question? Because the writer's life is, after all, part of his book.

*

If life and writing are rooted solely and deeply in freedom, then they are inextricably entwined.

*

Would the true writer be the one who can fuse his life with his characters' lives, real and imaginary, entities and abstractions, truth and lies? The one who fuses with us?

*

Is a writer sincere when, in his suffering, he wonders how he can express his suffering in words? Very definitely!

*

A writer: a liar of absolute honesty.

*

A game: invent the author from a reading of his books.

*

To write is to say "I am guilty." Guilty of having written, of being contemporary with the world, of having seen farther than others. The world in general cannot stand for this. The task of the powers that govern us – and they can now find their servants in the media to carry out these vile tasks – is to eliminate, in the name of everyone, the monster known as the writer. (The politically correct movement is but another avatar of this task of repressing writers since time immemorial.)

*

How often is it possible to measure the allergic reaction to writers, the aversion and intolerance, at its true level?

*

The writer is the possessor of a secret, the secret of writing. And for that, he will always be persecuted like a criminal or a thief.

*

What makes a writer write in a certain way, the way that fascinates, disturbs and worries us – and which the powers that be find so intolerable? The writer's singularity lies in his disturbing strangeness by itself.

*

Portrait of the writer: ambitious and modest, attentive and distracted, a toiler and a virtuoso, communicative and withdrawn, trusting and skeptical, depressive and exalted, gentle and cruel, amusing and serious, emotional and glacial, cold and melancholic, cheery and gloomy, generous and possessive, kind and rude, proper and vulgar, free and committed, light and heavy, upright and vile, fair and unjust, lyrical and prosaic, naive and sly, careful and sloppy, original and dull, conservative and revolutionary, idealist and realist, romantic and satirical, sentimental and cynical, witty and boring, sociable and reclusive, nostalgic and modern, healthy and ill, tender and tyrannical, timid and a show-off . . .

*

The writer is excessive, complex, and a web of contradictions. In sum, not someone to be frequented!

*

A writer is such a strange creature! Writing is such a curious profession!

*

A writer is probably the person, more than anyone else, who is leery of words.

*

Singularity is an act of revolt, a refusal to submit. The writer is *a rebel without a cause.*

*

Does being a writer predispose one to unhappiness?

*

It is unbearable to all that the writer is beyond our common destiny. "Far from the paths of murderers," as Kafka said so superbly.

*

Because the writer invents his language, he enters into direct conflict with society.

*

The fact that writers exist should definitely – and I mean this – be disturbing.

*

To write means freedom. I know this is a cliché, and yet what a profound truth is expressed therein; a truth we refuse to see!

*

The writer is a man without a country rather than a man without a party.

*

A writer can always say: "I am not from here."

*

Writers *live* their words under our very eyes. And therefore they live in a different fashion. Is a writer's life his work? Or his work, his life? A book like a life for his life? A book for the book his life is? All these are true. Literature, therefore, remains the only life to live.

*

Accept books, accept works of art, because we are for
the emotion of living.

There comes a time in writing when I can obey my prior texts, let myself be carried along by them so I can go forward and in what direction. I can't ignore them even though I know they don't tell me anything — anything concrete or good or beautiful.

*

All through my books I find: " I don't know."

*

The risk in writing: the invention of a new language no one will understand. Years will have to go by before it can be "translated"!

*

I wrote my books in near disorder, modifying the initial project as my writing progressed even though it was rigorously precise at the outset; because one word called forth another, I proceeded by association of ideas and metaphors; my reading of a book of fiction or an essay could reshape the formal purpose even if I had pursued it for an extensive time; I have written my books in much the same way one edits a film, through trial and error, comparing results, adjusting and modifying; the reading in public of certain of my texts could influence me to rewrite them . . . (The passage of time is a great help to the writer. He must not only be durable but perdurable.)

*

Each book was a proposition, sometimes clear (this kind of book had the cinema as a "pre-text"), sometimes unfocused (as was the case with *On ne sait pas que cela a été écrit avant et après la grande maladie*) [We don't know that this was written before and after the great scourge], but always with the intention to make progress in poetry.

*

I don't comment much on the book I happen to be working on at a given time, mainly because most of the time I don't know where I'm going and what I'm doing (what lines I'm experimenting along); I wait until there is a first result I find valid, with texts I'm not too ashamed of, before I can talk about them, or show them to others, very excited and with my heart ready to run and hide, as though I had just been struck by lightning.

*

I don't immediately realize the extent of the influence of the book I wrote just before the one I happen to be working on now and how much it can help me in my evolution as a writer.

*

Like a painter who changes the format of his paintings, or a musician who shifts from opera to chamber music, I too like to change "forms."

*

When I first started as a writer I think my writing was
complicated; then it was complex. And now I'm simple — I mean the complexity is at another level, and
therefore any simplicity is a perverse trick and is simple in appearance only.

*

Ever since *Les Passions du samedi* [Saturday's Pas-
sions]*, each of my collections is a short novel that
won't admit it's one.

*

I say to myself: what if my repetitions, my returning
to texts already written, my reiterations, my grafting
of texts to other texts, what if my entire "method" of
writing and my "style" were simply a need to indicate
a continuity in my work, to find a springboard, a
starting point that will propel me forward and help
me evolve, the foundation to lean on . . .

*

What if my repetitions and my cross-referencing
showed a need for a dialogue with my books . . .

---

* A selection of these poems was translated by Daniel Sloate and published by Guernica Editions in 1986.

*

Because of these markers of recognition (repetitions, re-use of certain texts), I never feel too alone with my writings.

*

All my repetitions, all the passages I use and re-use are like lures to snare the reader and hold his attention, to condition him so he too finds himself in familiar surroundings (the recurrence of certain words is reassuring). But from a more subtle standpoint, another reason is to entrench the text in the mind.

*

Repetitions yes, redundancies no!

*

It would be interesting to explain my books by their "spontaneous generation."

*

A word like a dab of colour in a painting and which may occur in several places. The same holds true for the repetitions in my texts.

*

Repetition helps in never closing a poem and in directing it towards an unfinished state. It's a piece in a mosaic. (As I often say: "A poem never lives alone"; whence my reticence at including it in an anthology.)

*

My lexicon (some say it's limited) is made up of my favorite words. The words my texts offer the reader so he may divine the secret cipher to some impossible knowledge about me, the cipher of my otherness and therefore of my death. These words can only be the words I love.

*

I tell myself that I live an adventure every day I write. Writing always tests itself, always invents itself over and over. All this is very stimulating – you forget everything: the material conditions of publishing, the relations with the institution, the readers I won't reach . . .

*

I do believe writing has not made me reasonable. I detect a marked tendency in me to be increasingly rebellious and recalcitrant.

*

I like the phrase "create a book" because it suggests books are made or invented from nothing or next to nothing.

*

From one book to the next I have always been meticulous in giving priority to the careful crafting of my words.

*

I'm a very good worker when I write!

*

I have always looked upon my books as research on different forms.

*

I think it's possible to discern different periods in my work: pink, blue, red, black. The colours of words and the soul.

*

From one book to the next, I have tried to *revitalize* my texts, to revitalize Writing. There is an attempt in each of my books to return to the basic concept of "modern poetry" and decide whether it is apt and efficacious. To decide whether it's worthwhile to continue writing poetry. To decide whether it's worthwhile to go on living (living and writing are inseparable, like two love birds).

*

Continuing to write poetry is one way for me to remain loyal to the revelation that poetry, and Quebec poetry in particular, was for me over thirty years ago. Quebec poetry had *form* for me more than it had substance.

*

Form was definitely at the root of my desire to write, and it still is. Substance is the surface on which I disappear still.

*

My collections (*Le cycle des Passions*, *Nuits*, *L'accélérateur d'intensité*) [Cycle of the Passions, Nights, The Intensity Accelerator] gave me the opportunity to move ahead and begin working on a new series of projects. All past writings are like bends in the road leading to new ones.

*

The book I'm writing at present may exist in sketch form in the previous book (check and see if this is so).

*

When I compare the punctuation of my early books with the most recent, I realize I don't breathe the way I used to. My breathing is shorter. And my punctuation has become more "traditional," in the sense I can now do whatever I want between two periods!

*

Punctuation immediately brings music to my mind. The music of each book or series is very important to me. This work is a *ballade*, that one a cantata, another is a *fantaisie* and still another a waltz. (The seven parts of *On sait que cela a été écrit avant et après la grande maladie* [We know that this was written before and after the great scourge] are seven different musical forms).

*

Nicole Brossard and Roger Des Roches are still the two authors whom I think of the most when I write. My two deconstructors. Every one of their books becomes a writing program for me.

*

Now when I write, I'm much less terrorized (gentle, stimulating terror!) by the collections of poets of my generation: Des Roches, Charron, de Bellefeuille, Théoret.

*

I believe I've become less aware of the literary devices I use in my books — is this a case of the ego being often absent?

*

The impression deepens in me — and the inclination especially — that I write what I want to write and that I read criticism with but half an eye, because increasingly I intend to do what my heart tells me to do.

*

Why was my generation so obsessed by form?

*

The "demon" of form.

*

The "demon" of fragments also. (Responsible for the pleasure in keeping a notebook.) (The demon that was Barthes.)

*

In Barthes' *Plaisir du texte* [Pleasure of the Text], he hadn't yet succeeded, in 1973, in liberating us from the political clichés that threatened to engulf us and pit us all against one another as die-hard enemies (class enemies?) – and to turn us into full-fledged paranoids. But the job was done later in 1978 with his *Fragments d'un discours amoureux* [Fragments of an Amorous Discourse]. And whom do I mean by "us"? On the whole, I'm speaking of the generation of Les Herbes rouges.

*

Of the two "tutelary gods" of the time, Freud and Mao, both of whom I had quoted textually in one of my collections (*D'un corps à l'autre*) [From One Body to Another], Freud is the only one to survive – because he was the greater of the two.

*

Les Herbes rouges, neither a clan nor a coterie. Rather, an informal group that accomplished a slow revolution in poetic language; a revolution that was composed of refusals and attacks, audacity and hesitation, research and rivalry (indeed, it seems to me there were many rivalries).

*

Like any group that has caused an upheaval in artistic or literary history (think of surrealism in literature, impressionism in painting, the New Wave in the cinema), and despite what others may think, we will remember the names of the authors of Les Herbes rouges because they imposed another kind of poetry and other forms on their literary domain. And like any group in its temporal context, its members were accused of causing upheavals and of declaring a new esthetics based on rejection of the status quo and a breaking away from it. Seen from this perspective, I am quite sure of the importance of Les Herbes rouges.

November 1992-April 1994

AGMV Marquis

MEMBER OF THE SCABRINI GROUP

Quebec, Canada
2001